Clone
Alone

'Clone Alone'
An original concept by Katie Dale
© Katie Dale

Illustrated by Duc Nguyen

Published by MAVERICK ARTS PUBLISHING LTD

Studio 11, City Business Centre, 6 Brighton Road,

Horsham, West Sussex, RH13 5BB

© Maverick Arts Publishing Limited August 2021

+44 (0)1403 256941

A CIP catalogue record for this book is available at the British Library.

ISBN 978-1-84886-805-2

www.maverickbooks.co.uk

Grey

This book is rated as: Grey Band (Guided Reading)

Clone Alone

Written by
Katie Dale

Illustrated by
Duc Nguyen

Chapter 1

"We're here!"

J3264 fizzed with excitement as he and his three hundred thousand clone brothers crammed against the windows of the Mother Ship.

"Let me see!" J3264 begged, struggling to see anything through the throng. Finally the crowds parted and he caught a glimpse of the planet below. His five eyes widened in wonder. For there was Earth: a swirling blue and green sphere, glowing in the darkness. He had never seen anything more beautiful.

"I can't believe the humans are destroying such a perfect planet," he sighed. "Don't they know how lucky they are?"

"Not that lucky—we're about to wipe them all out!" H3876 commented, beside him.

"They'll be wiped out anyway when they kill the Earth," J3264 reasoned. "But at least we can save the planet and look after it properly. I can't believe we've finally found a new home!" He beamed. "After seven thousand light years searching, I'd almost given up hope!"

H3876 grinned. "Never give up hope!"

"Attention!" the Commander yelled suddenly, and the clones fell silent. "It is time for the launch-first lottery!"

J3264 crossed his four red tentacles and twelve green toes. *Pick me! Pick me!* he wished silently. He loved his brothers, but living on a ship with three hundred thousand clones who all looked exactly the same, J3264 sometimes felt a bit... anonymous. He yearned to do something special with his life, to make a difference. Maybe today was his lucky day, the day he would finally be singled out for something important...

"The clone chosen to launch his space pod first is..."

J3264 held his breath.

"H3876!"

J3264 sighed heavily, then forced a smile for his brother. "Congratulations!"

H3876 grinned at him. "You want this more than me," he said, quickly swapping their name badges. "You go instead. No one will ever know."

J3264 stared at him in amazement. "Are you sure?"

"H3876, where are you?" the Commander yelled, gazing out at the three hundred thousand identical clones.

H3876 grinned and pushed J3264 forwards. "He's here!"

The Commander's frown relaxed. "Finally! Everyone take your positions!"

As everyone jumped into their space pods, J3264 hurried to the front. He flashed H3876 a grateful smile. For once, he was glad they all looked alike! Now he finally had a chance to do something important!

"Begin countdown! 5... 4..."

J3264's tentacles tingled with nerves and excitement.

He couldn't believe he'd be the first to land on Earth!
How exciting!

"3, 2, 1... INVADE!"

J3264 zoomed towards the
Earth. The closer he got,
the more beautiful it
looked. Pinpricks of
light became cities,
then buildings, then

BANG!

There was a loud explosion!
BANG! BANG! BANG!
Hundreds of coloured sparks
filled the sky all around, shaking
the space pod with their loud noises.

WHIRR! WHIZZ! POP! BANG!

J3264's four hearts beat fast. What was going on?

"The humans are attacking!" the Commander's voice crackled through J3264's headphones. "Retreat!"

His pulse racing, J3264 hurriedly turned his space pod around to return to the Mother Ship.

But suddenly—

SMASH!

Blinding light filled his vision and his space pod lurched violently.

"Help!" he called into his communicator. "My space pod's been hit!"

The pod spiralled wildly out of control, alarms blaring all around him. His tentacles scrambled over the buttons desperately, but it was no use.

"Help! Please!" he yelled again—but then he noticed the communicator light was off. It must have been damaged when his space pod got hit. No one could hear him! They were all leaving without him!

"No!" J3264 screamed helplessly, watching his brothers' space pods whizz off out of sight, as he and his broken pod tumbled helplessly towards the Earth.

Chapter 2

CRASH!

J3264's space pod hurtled straight into a tall tree, tumbled to the ground, rolled down a large hill, and landed in a huge pile of something soft and white.

"Eurrrrrgh!" he groaned, his head spinning. Then he gasped. "I'm alive!" He checked all his tentacles. "I'm not even hurt!"

He tried to start the space pod, but it was no good. "But I am stranded," he sighed.

He opened the door, and peered out nervously. J3264 had been created on the Mother Ship. He'd never been on a planet before. He took a deep breath, swallowed hard, and tentatively stepped outside... and immediately slipped over! His feet shot out from underneath him and he slid over with a bump, landing in cold white wet stuff.

"Ouch!" he cried, and the sound echoed strangely. J3264 gazed around him and could see nothing but trees. He shivered. He had never, not even for the tiniest millisecond of his whole entire life, been alone. With three hundred thousand clone brothers, life was usually so crammed and noisy and squashed that he used to wish he could be by himself sometimes.

But now here he was, all alone on a very cold strange planet.

It was too quiet, too still... Until it wasn't!

"Krish!" a voice yelled, breaking the silence. "Wait for me!"

J3264 panicked. Humans were coming! He hastily covered his space pod with more white stuff, then hid behind it as two small humans ran into the clearing.

"I'm sure the shooting star must've landed near here," the human who was mostly blue and quite hairy said. "It was so close!"

"It was a meteor, not a shooting star—and look!" the other one (who was less hairy and mostly green) cried, pointing towards J3264.

Oh no! Had it seen him? He ducked.

"Footprints!" the blue human squealed.

"They're the strangest footprints I've ever seen!" The green one frowned. "I wonder what animal could've made them?"

"Let's follow them and find out!"

Oh no! J3264 panicked. He couldn't run away, or they'd follow his footprints, but he couldn't let them see him either! At least not in his true form...

Quickly, he pressed the cloaking device on his spacesuit, hoping against hope that it hadn't been too badly damaged in the crash...

"Oh!" the green human appeared in front of J3264 and gasped.

J3264 froze. Had the cloaking device worked?

"What is it?" the blue human called, rounding the corner. "Oh! A boy! Hi!"

J3264 sighed with relief. The cloaking device must have worked. He looked like a human!

"Hi!" he replied. Thank goodness the Commander made them learn all the human languages before invading!

"I'm Sanvi, and this is my brother, Krish," the blue human said. "What's your name?"

"Um... J—" J3264 stopped himself just in time. He couldn't tell them his real name, but he couldn't think of any human names!

This was a disaster!

"Nice to meet you, Jay!" Krish grinned.

J3264 sighed with relief. How lucky that Jay was a human name!

"Did you come to see the fireworks too?" Sanvi asked.

Jay blinked. "Fireworks?"

"You must have seen them—they filled the sky!" she beamed. "I think they're my favourite thing about New Year celebrations!"

"Plus it's the one night of the year we're allowed to stay up till midnight!" Krish grinned.

Jay smiled. So the humans weren't attacking them after all—the explosions were their strange way of celebrating a special day! He had to tell his brothers! But how? His communicator was broken!

"Did you see the shooting star?" Sanvi asked.

"She means meteor," Krish corrected.

J3264 shook his head, edging in front of the space pod. Luckily it was hidden by the white stuff.

"Krish! Sanvi! There you are!" Two bigger humans ran into the clearing, and Jay backed away. He suddenly felt very outnumbered.

"Mum! Dad! We couldn't find the meteor, but we did find a new friend!" Sanvi said. "This is Jay."

"Nice to meet you, Jay," the biggest human said, smiling. "Do you live around here?"

Jay shook his head.

Krish frowned. "Are you lost?"

Jay hesitated, then nodded.

"Don't worry," Sanvi said. "We'll help you find your way home."

"I... I don't have a home," Jay said.

"That's terrible!" Sanvi gasped. "We'll help you—won't we, Mum and Dad?"

The two big humans smiled at each other.

"Of course we'll help you find a home," the hairier one said. "Till then, you can stay with us."

"If you want to," the other big human added.

They all looked at Jay, but he hesitated. After all, he and his brothers had come to take the humans' planet and wipe them out—how could he stay with them?

But his space pod was broken, he had no way of getting home or contacting his brothers, he was stranded on a strange planet, and he was colder than he'd ever imagined. He needed to devise a plan to get back to the Mother Ship... but right now he was too cold to think properly.

"Th-thank you," he smiled, nodding.

Chapter 3

The humans' house was very strange. It wasn't made of metal, and it didn't fly. In fact, it didn't move at all. But at least it was warm and dry.

"You must be hungry, Jay," one of the big humans—Mum—smiled, and Jay nodded eagerly. But instead of eating paste from a tube, like Jay was used to, they gave him strange solid food.

Then, when Sanvi finally gave him a tube of stripy food upstairs, she looked at him very oddly as he squeezed it into his mouth and ate it—then she brushed it on her teeth and spat it out! Weird!

Weirder still, the humans stripped off their colourful skin and swapped it for a different one when they went to bed—and gave Jay another skin to put on too! Bizarre!

It was all very strange. And Jay felt strange too. He was used to fitting in, to being exactly the same as everyone else, but here he felt out of place for the first time in his life. He'd always wanted to be special, to be different in some way. But now he was, he didn't like it. He missed his brothers terribly.

He gazed out of the window at the star-filled night sky. But there was no sign of the Mother Ship. Had they left without him? Would he ever see his clone brothers again?

The next morning, Jay opened his eyes and gasped.

"What's happened?" he cried, gazing around the brightly-lit room. "The light's too strong! Turn it off!"

Krish sat up in his bunk bed and laughed. "Turn off the sun? Good one, Jay!"

Jay frowned. "The sun?"

Sanvi jumped out of bed and pulled back a piece of

cloth at the window and the room got even brighter.

"What a beautiful day!" she beamed.

Jay gasped as he looked outside. The Earth looked the same as last night, but different too—all the colours were brighter, the white stuff sparkled and glistened, and strange creatures fluttered from tree to tree.

"Beautiful!" he agreed, smiling.

The humans continued to be weird. They spat their tube food out again, then went downstairs.

"Cereal or porridge?" Mum asked.

"Um..." Jay hesitated, then saw Sanvi pour little hoops into a bowl. She noticed him watching and offered him the box.

"Have you tried this cereal?" she grinned. "It's yummy!"

Jay took the box and smiled nervously. "Thanks." He tipped some hoops into a bowl then picked one up, sniffed it, and took a bite. It was very hard, dry and crunchy. He grimaced.

"Don't you want any soy milk?" Sanvi laughed, passing him a jug of white liquid.

"Oh," Jay said, taking it. "Thank you." He drank from the jug. It was much nicer than hard hoops.

"No!" Sanvi burst out laughing. "Pour it on your cereal!"

"Haven't you ever had cereal before?" Krish chuckled, pouring milk on his hoops then using a metal device to shovel them into his mouth.

Jay did his best to copy. The crunchy hoops were much nicer with milk. In fact, they were delicious! He couldn't wait to tell his brothers all about it... but how?

Suddenly Jay spotted a metal box with an antenna by the sink—it must be a communicator! Maybe he could use it to contact the Mother Ship! When Krish and Sanvi went to change colour—again—Jay crept over to the communicator and turned it on. Immediately loud strange noises filled the room. Oh no! Was it an alarm?

Sanvi and Krish hurried in and Jay panicked. But the humans didn't seem angry. Strangely, they were smiling, and, stranger still, they both started moving oddly.

"Are—are you okay?" Jay asked Sanvi anxiously as she whirled around the room. "What are you doing?"

"Dancing!" she laughed. "I love this song! Come and dance with us, Jay!"

Jay frowned. What was 'dancing'?

"Move your hips like this!" Krish cried, wiggling from side to side.

"Jump up and down like this!" Sanvi added, leaping in the air.

"Um... why?" Jay asked.

"It's fun!" they laughed.

Jay wanted to fit in, so he tried his best to copy them. It felt very strange and unnatural at first, but Sanvi and Krish grabbed his hands and as they all moved together in time with the noises it started to feel... good!

He felt something strange bubble inside him. "Ha ha ha!" He was laughing! Jay blinked. He'd never laughed before! It felt great!

Then Mum walked in. "Bad news, Jay," she sighed. "I can't get in touch with anyone to help find you a home today. It's New Year's Day, so most places are closed, but you can stay with us as long as you need to."

"I'm glad he can stay longer!" Sanvi said, grinning.

"Me too!" said Krish. "We're having fun!"

Jay smiled at Krish and Sanvi, and nodded. Humans may be very odd... but they were kind, and fun.

Then his smile slipped as he remembered he and his brothers were planning to wipe them all out... He had to get back to his space pod and try to contact the Mother Ship!

Chapter 4

Jay tried to sneak back to the pod without Sanvi and Krish noticing, but his snowy footprints gave him away yet again.

"There you are!" Sanvi cried, running up behind him. "Where are you going?"

"Um… just for a walk," Jay fibbed.

"Great idea!" Krish grinned. "We'll join you. It's beautiful outside!"

But as they wandered down the street, discarded cans and wrappers and plastic bags spoiled the beautiful countryside.

"They must be left over from last night's New Year's Eve parties," Krish sighed.

Jay frowned. How could humans be so careless and destructive? He and his brothers would take much better care of Earth.

"I know!" Sanvi said. "Let's pick it all up!"

Jay stared at her. "You want to pick up other people's rubbish?"

Sanvi nodded. "If we don't, who will? We all need to do our part to save the planet."

Jay's eyes widened. "You're trying to save the Earth?"

"Of course!" Krish said. "There's lots of things we can do to help."

Jay's jaw dropped. He thought humans were destroying the Earth, not looking after it... but maybe the situation was more complex than he'd thought?

"Come on, let's see who can pick up the most litter in an hour!" Sanvi cried. "It'll be fun!"

Krish nodded, grinning. "Ready, steady, go!"

After an hour, Jay's bag was the fullest.

"You win, Jay!" Krish grinned.

"And now wildlife won't eat or get stuck in any litter," Sanvi beamed. "We're all winners—especially the Earth!"

Jay's smile broadened. Sanvi and Krish certainly seemed to be trying to help save their planet.

They showed Jay how to sort the litter and recycle as much as possible. They explained that eating fewer animal products helped save the rainforests and reduce harmful emissions. They walked or cycled whenever possible, tried not to use disposable plastics, and made sure they turned water and electricity off whenever it wasn't being used.

"But you're just two small humans—er, I mean people," Jay said. "What difference can you make?"

"Every person makes a difference," Krish said. "And it's not just us. All our family and friends are trying to help too."

Sanvi nodded. "We all have to do our best."

Jay stared at them both, impressed. If only his own people had done the same thousands of years ago, maybe their planet wouldn't have died...

Sanvi smiled. "If we all work together, we can save the Earth. It isn't too late."

Jay swallowed hard. He really hoped it *wasn't* too late! He had to contact his clone brothers and tell them not to invade after all! Humans deserved a second chance!

He turned on his heel and ran away through the snow.

"Jay—wait!" Krish called. But Jay couldn't wait—there was no time to lose!

Jay ran all the way to his space pod. Some of the snow had melted in the morning sunshine, revealing the door and roof sticking out of the mound. He hurried inside and picked up the communicator.

"Please work!" he begged, pressing lots of buttons. "J3264 to Mother Ship, can you hear me?"

There was no response. "Mother Ship! Are you there? Can anybody hear me?"

"We can," came a voice—but it wasn't from Jay's communicator.

He whirled round to find Sanvi and Krish staring at him, their eyes wide as flying saucers.

"Is that a... a spaceship?" Krish gasped, stepping closer.

"What's going on, Jay?" Sanvi frowned.

Jay sighed. "My name isn't Jay. It's J3264. I'm a clone from Planet Xiffon." He pressed a button on his spacesuit and instantly returned to his true appearance.

Sanvi squealed and Krish backed away. "You're an... an alien?"

Jay nodded.

"The meteor..." Krish said slowly. "It was you, wasn't it?"

Jay nodded. "My space pod got hit by the fireworks and I crash-landed."

"You poor thing!" Sanvi cried. "Is that how you lost your family?"

Jay nodded.

"Don't worry, we'll help you get home!" Sanvi said kindly.

"Wait a minute," Krish said, frowning. "What were you and the other aliens doing here? Did you come to invade Earth?"

"Oh Krish, you're so suspicious!" Sanvi laughed. "Jay's our friend! They obviously came in peace, didn't you, Jay?"

Jay gulped and Sanvi's smile faltered.

Krish folded his arms. "It's time you told us everything."

Chapter 5

Krish and Sanvi listened, wide-eyed, as Jay told them all about his dead planet and his people's epic search for a new home, and how they thought Earth would be perfect.

"So you were just going to wipe us out and take our planet?!" Krish exclaimed angrily.

"We thought we'd be rescuing Earth from the creatures who were destroying it," Jay explained. "I didn't know there were people like you trying to save the planet."

Sanvi frowned. "But now you do."

Jay nodded. "That's why I was trying to communicate with the Mother Ship—to call off the invasion! But my communicator was broken in the crash."

"I'm calling the police!" Krish said, storming off.

"Krish! You can't!" Sanvi cried, hurrying after him. "Who knows what the police would do to Jay! They might lock him up—or worse!"

Jay gulped.

"I don't care!" Krish yelled. "Jay and his brothers were going to wipe us out! Whatever the police do to him won't be as bad as erasing an entire species!"

"But humans have wiped out loads of species too!" Sanvi countered. "Dodos, Great Auks, Cape Lions, Javan Tigers—"

"That's not the same!" Krish argued. "We didn't *deliberately* wipe them out!"

"I'm just saying I can understand why the clones thought they might be helping Earth by getting rid of humans," Sanvi said. "We have caused a lot of damage."

"I know," Krish frowned. "But we're trying to fix it!"

"Exactly, and that's what Jay's trying to do now—to stop the invasion before it's too late!" Sanvi cried. "We're on the same team, Krish. We have to stick together and try to find a way to fix Jay's communicator, not blame each other or go running off to the police!"

Jay stared from Krish to Sanvi, amazed that two creatures of the same species could be so different. He and his clone brothers always thought and did exactly the same things... but maybe if they didn't, if they argued and debated and discussed different ideas instead... their planet would still be alive.

Krish looked conflicted as he looked from Sanvi to Jay... then suddenly his frown deepened, and he sprinted off between the trees.

"Oh no!" Jay cried anxiously. "Is he going to fetch the police?"

"I don't know," Sanvi sighed heavily. "Come on, let's fix this communicator—quick!"

Chapter 6

Sanvi hurriedly fetched her toolkit and frowned hard as she tinkered with the communicator. Jay watched anxiously, crossing his tentacles tight.

Finally the communicator made a crackling sound. Jay's five eyes lit up. Was it working?

"Try it now!" Sanvi said, handing it to him excitedly.

"Hello?" Jay said in Xiffonese. "Can you hear me?" He listened carefully.

"Hello?" came a voice. "J3264, is that you? H3876 told us about the switch. Are you okay?"

"Yes!" Jay cried. "I'm fine! But you must not invade the Earth!"

He grinned at Sanvi, who beamed back. They'd done it! They'd stopped the invasion!

"Hello?" the voice said again. "J3264, can you hear me?"

"Yes!" Jay said anxiously. "Did you hear me? Don't invade!" He waited for a long moment, Sanvi watching nervously.

The communicator crackled again. "J3264, we can't hear you. If you can hear us, don't worry. We have tracked your space pod and will rescue you tonight..."

"Hurray!" Jay cried.

"...when we invade Earth!"

"NOOOO!" Jay yelled.

"What happened?" Sanvi asked anxiously.

"They couldn't hear me," Jay sighed. "It didn't work!"

"Then we have to improve the signal somehow!" Sanvi said. "And quick!"

"It's too late—Krish is back!" Jay cried, pointing.

Sanvi whirled round to see her brother. But instead of bringing the police—he'd brought a sledge!

"I figured we'd need to get the space pod to higher ground to get a good signal," Krish grinned.

"Oh Krish, thank you!" Sanvi threw her arms around him happily. "I knew we were on the same team!"

Jay beamed.

Together, they loaded the space pod onto the sledge and dragged it up the snowy hill.

"Try the communicator again now," Sanvi said, when they reached the top.

Jay climbed inside the space pod. "Hello?" he said into the communicator. "Hello, can you hear me?"

Sanvi and Krish crossed their fingers and Jay crossed all his tentacles.

The communicator crackled.

"J3264!" came a voice. "We can hear you!"

"Thank goodness!" He grinned at Sanvi and Krish, who high-fived happily.

"Don't invade Earth!" Jay continued hurriedly. "The humans are trying to save the planet, not destroy it!"

There was a long pause.

"J3264, you are wrong. Humans have devastated the planet with their litter, pollution, waste, greed and carelessness."

"Yes, but now they're trying to save it!" Jay insisted.

"Some may be," the Commander said. "But not everyone. Not enough."

"Please!" Jay begged. "Can we at least take a vote?"

"A vote?" the commander said. "We do not need a vote. We are clones. We all think the same."

"I don't!" Jay insisted. "Maybe others disagree too!"

"Fine," the Commander said. "All those in favour of invading Earth, say INVADE!"

"INVADE!"

The noise was so deafening, Krish and Sanvi covered their ears.

"Everyone except you voted to invade," the Commander said. "You are out-voted three hundred thousand to one. We will invade tonight!"

Chapter 7

"That's that, then," Krish said glumly.

"At least we tried," Sanvi sighed. "But it's hopeless."

Jay sighed heavily. Then he remembered what H3876 said: *'Never give up hope!'*

Jay gritted his teeth. "I'm not giving up."

"But what can we do against three hundred thousand alien clones?" Krish asked.

"Make a difference, that's what!" Jay cried. "Like you both said. Every person makes a difference!"

Krish and Sanvi looked up.

"You and your family are making a difference by helping clean up the Earth," said Jay. "Now it's my turn.

Clones are used to following orders and not thinking for themselves. I have to change that!" He picked up the communicator again.

"My brothers, listen to me," Jay said. "We cannot wipe out an entire species! It's wrong!"

"Humans have wiped out many species!" the Commander retorted.

"Not deliberately!" Jay argued. "If you deliberately wipe them out, you're no better than they are! In fact, you're worse! No species has the right to deliberately wipe out another! Please," Jay begged. "Give them a second chance!"

"The humans are destroying their planet!" The Commander said. "They don't deserve a second chance."

"*We* destroyed *our* planet," Jay retaliated. "Maybe it's *us* that don't deserve a second chance—especially if that chance is only possible if we wipe out another species. How could we ever live with ourselves?!"

There was a long pause.

"But we've learned from our mistakes," Jay continued. "We know what we did wrong, and we know how to save a planet. We can help the humans save Earth."

The clones were silent for a long time.

"Has the communicator stopped working again?" Krish asked anxiously.

Jay held his breath. Had the clones heard him? Would they even listen, if they had? No clone had ever spoken against the Commander like that. Would they go ahead with the invasion and wipe him out too, for disobeying?

Then, slowly, there came the sound of clapping. Sanvi and Krish looked at Jay. The sound grew louder and louder until finally it was almost deafening.

Jay beamed at Sanvi and Krish. But would it be enough to convince the Commander?

"J3264," said the Commander finally. "We are a peaceful species. Above all, we want to save the Earth. If the humans want that too, if we can help them... then that is what we should do. You have convinced us."

The clones burst into deafening cheers and applause.

"It worked!" Jay gasped in delighted disbelief.

"Hurray!" Sanvi squealed.

"You did it!" Krish gasped. "You actually did it!"

"We did it together," Jay beamed. "You two have taught me so much. Thank you."

"We're all winners," Sanvi grinned.

"Especially the Earth," Krish beamed. "Group hug!"

Jay had never been hugged before. It felt amazing! His four hearts swelled with relief, joy, and love. He'd defended his new friends, stood up to his clone brothers, saved a species and a planet! He'd finally made a difference.

Discussion Points

1. Why did Jay want to win the launch-first lottery?

2. What caused Jay to crash-land on Earth?

a) A rocket

b) Fireworks

c) His spaceship malfunctioned

3. What was your favourite part of the story?

4. What do Sanvi and Krish do that shows Jay they care about the planet?

5. Why do you think the alien clones change their minds about invading Earth?

6. Who was your favourite character and why?

7. There were moments in the story when Jay had to **put himself in someone else's position**. Where do you think the story shows this most?

8. What do you think happens after the end of the story?

Book Bands for Guided Reading

The Institute of Education book banding system is a scale of colours that reflects the various levels of reading difficulty. The bands are assigned by taking into account the content, the language style, the layout and phonics. Word, phrase and sentence level work is also taken into consideration.

The Maverick Readers Scheme is a bright, attractive range of books covering the pink to grey bands. All of these books have been book banded for guided reading to the industry standard and edited by a leading educational consultant.

To view the whole Maverick Readers scheme, visit our website at

www.maverickearlyreaders.com

Or scan the QR code to view our scheme instantly!

Maverick Chapter Readers
(From Lime to Grey Band)